Ark
Adventures

Noah and his wife think a flood
might be coming, so they have built
a big boat called the Ark. They are
sailing around the world to rescue the
animals before it starts to rain.

Let's all go on an animal adventure!

For Hannah Etherington
S.G.

For Agatha
A.P.

Reading Consultant: Prue Goodwin, Lecturer in literacy and children's books

ORCHARD BOOKS
338 Euston Road, London NW1 3BH
Orchard Books Australia
Level 17/207 Kent Street, Sydney, NSW 2000

First published in 2011
First paperback publication in 2012

ISBN 978 1 40830 554 6 (hardback)
ISBN 978 1 40830 562 1 (paperback)

Text © Sally Grindley 2011
Illustrations © Alex Paterson 2011

A CIP catalogue record for this book is available from the British Library.

1 3 5 7 9 10 8 6 4 2 (hardback)
3 5 7 9 10 8 6 4 2 (paperback)

Printed in China

Orchard Books is a division of Hachette Children's Books,
an Hachette UK company.

Crazy
Chameleons!

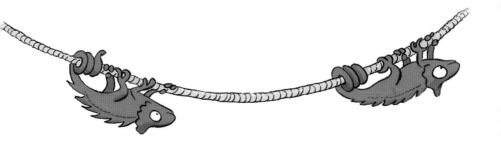

Written by Sally Grindley

Illustrated by Alex Paterson

ORCHARD

"Where are we going today, Noah?"
asked Mrs Noah one sunny morning.

"To Madagascar!" said Noah.

Noah looked in their *Big Book of Animals.* "We can find chameleons and lemurs there."

"How exciting!" said Mrs Noah.

Noah read on. "It says that chameleons are *very* good at hiding."

"That's all right," said Mrs Noah.
"You like playing hide-and-seek."
"And it says that lemurs can be *very*
naughty," said Noah.
"Oh dear," said Mrs Noah.

They looked out as the Ark sailed
towards the shore. Just then, two
lemurs ran across the beach.
"Look how they stick their tails
in the air!" cried Noah.
"They do look *very* naughty,"
said Mrs Noah.

The Ark reached the shore and Noah lowered the gangplank.

Before he could step down onto the beach, the lemurs ran past him and jumped onto the roof of the Ark. "That's good," Noah laughed. "They want to come with us."

"They can't stay up there,"
Mrs Noah cried.

The lemurs leapt up and down and waved their tails.

"They are *very* naughty," said Noah.

"I'll go and settle them in, while you find the chameleons," sighed Mrs Noah.

Noah changed into his jungle clothes.
He left the Ark and hurried across
the sand.

When he reached the jungle,
Noah stopped.

"I hope I don't meet any spiders."
He shivered. "Mrs Noah doesn't mind
creepy-crawlies, but I don't like them."

Noah pushed his way through
the bushes.

It was noisy and damp inside the
jungle, and very, very dark.

Something ran across Noah's feet.

"Argh! What was that?" he cried.

Something brushed against his face.

"Eek! I don't like it in here!"

he wailed.

Suddenly, a ray of sunlight shone through the trees. It lit up something red and shiny on a branch in front of Noah.

The red thing winked at him.

"What's that?" he squealed.

It turned green and winked again.

"A chameleon!" Noah gasped.

The sun went in and the chameleon disappeared.

"I can't see you!" said Noah.

Two more eyes winked at him, then disappeared again.

"Are you playing hide-and-seek?" Noah chuckled.

Noah hid behind a tree and waited.
When the sun shone again, he looked
round the tree.

A pink chameleon was tiptoeing
along a branch in front of him.

Noah jumped out. "I've found you!" he cried.

The chameleon winked a big wink.
Then suddenly Noah couldn't see it
any more.

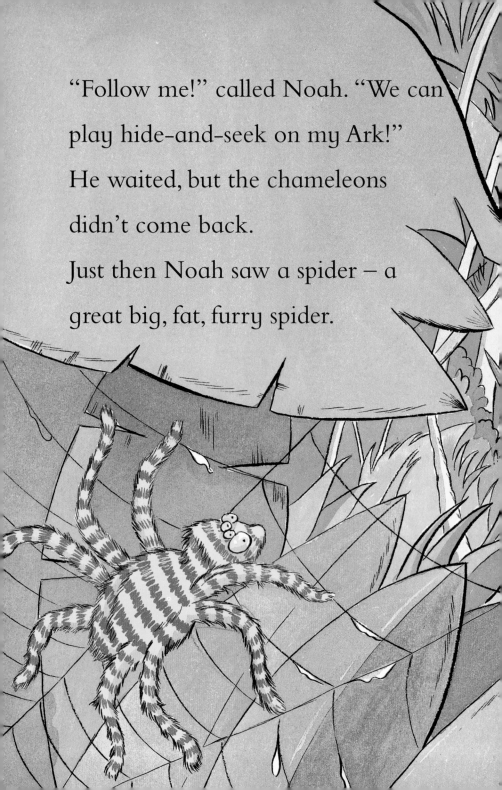

"Follow me!" called Noah. "We can play hide-and-seek on my Ark!" He waited, but the chameleons didn't come back.

Just then Noah saw a spider – a great big, fat, furry spider.

"Help!" cried Noah, and he ran back
through the jungle as fast as he could.

Mrs Noah waved to him as he ran towards the Ark. "Did you find any chameleons?" she asked.

"I found some, but they kept hiding from me!" panted Noah.

"What's that on your shoulder?"
asked Mrs Noah.
Noah squealed. "Is it a spider?
Get rid of it!"

Mrs Noah leant towards him and gently picked up two chameleons. "Are these what you've been looking for?" she said.

"Well I never!" said Noah.

The chameleons winked at him.

"We'll have to keep an eye on them,"

chuckled Mrs Noah.

"How are the lemurs?" asked Noah.
Just as he spoke, the two lemurs
jumped down and ran off with
his hat.

"Hey!" exclaimed Noah.

"They've been *very* naughty,"
sighed Mrs Noah.

"Never mind," smiled Noah. "Now,
where *have* those chameleons gone?"

SALLY GRINDLEY · ALEX PATERSON

Crazy Chameleons!   978 1 40830 562 1

Giant Giraffes!   978 1 40830 563 8

Too-slow Tortoises!   978 1 40830 564 5

Kung Fu Kangaroos!   978 1 40830 565 2

Playful Penguins!   978 1 40830 566 9

Pesky Sharks!   978 1 40830 567 6

Cheeky Chimpanzees!   978 1 40830 568 3

Hungry Bears!   978 1 40830 569 0

All priced at £4.99

Orchard Books are available from all good bookshops, or can be
ordered from our website: www.orchardbooks.co.uk,
or telephone 01235 827702, or fax 01235 827703.